For Okie

This is a work of fiction. Names, characters, places, and incidents either are
the product of the author's imagination or are used fictitiously.
Any resemblance to actual persons, living or dead, events, or locales is entirely coincidental.

Published in the United States by Random House Children's Books,
a division of Random House, Inc., New York.
Originally published in a slightly different form by the authors in 2004.

www.randomhouse.com/kids
Educators and librarians, for a variety of teaching tools, visit us at
www.randomhouse.com/teachers

Library of Congress Cataloging-in-Publication Data
O'Connor, Joe.
Where did Daddy's hair go? / by Joe O'Connor ; illustrated by Henry Payne.
p. cm.
SUMMARY: When Jeremiah overhears his father talking about
losing his hair, Jeremiah sets out to find it.
ISBN 0-375-83571-7 (trade) — ISBN 0-375-93571-1 (lib. bdg.)
[1. Baldness—Fiction. 2. Hair—Fiction.] I. Payne, Henry, ill. II. Title.
PZ7.O22234Whe 2006   [E]—dc22   2005005485

PRINTED IN CHINA   First Random House Edition   10 9 8 7 6 5 4 3 2 1

RANDOM HOUSE and colophon are registered trademarks of Random House, Inc.

Where Did Daddy's Hair Go?

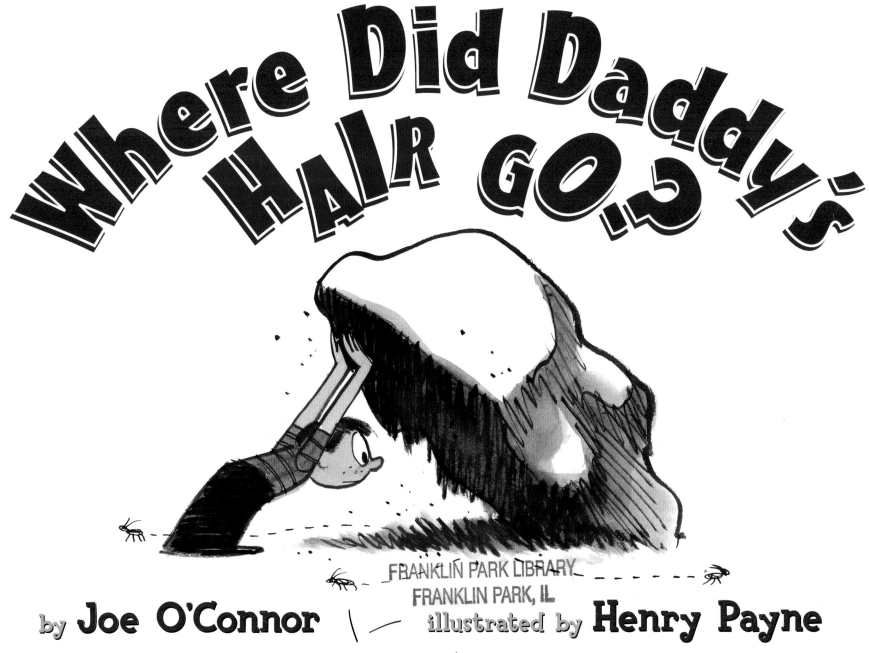

by **Joe O'Connor**   illustrated by **Henry Payne**

RANDOM HOUSE 🏠 NEW YORK

OUTFIELD
SEATS

Jeremiah Jensen was very excited. It was a bright, sunny day at the ballpark, and he was at his first big-league baseball game with his daddy.

Jeremiah had never seen so many people in one place!

Jeremiah's dad was also feeling good. He was with his son, enjoying the smells of the ballpark and watching his favorite team—just as he had done so many times with his own father, Jeremiah's grandpa.

The score was tied 0-0 when suddenly there was the crack of a bat. One of the home-team players had hit a home run! Jeremiah's dad jumped up from his seat and cheered loudly for his team.

Just then, a large man seated behind them yelled,

"HEY, BALDY—SIT DOWN!"

Jeremiah was startled—and a little worried.

But with a smile, his dad turned to the man and said,

"How did you know my name?"

The large man smiled back.

Later, as they were driving home from the game, Jeremiah thought again about the large man. "Daddy, why did that man call you Baldy?"

His dad smiled. "Because people who don't have much hair on their heads are considered bald," he explained.

Jeremiah thought about this. Then he wondered what

he might look like

without hair.

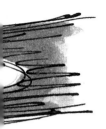

The next day, Jeremiah was sitting at the kitchen table with his dad. His dad was on the phone.

Jeremiah wasn't paying much attention to what his father was saying, but he *did* hear one thing: "**Ever since I lost my hair...**"

Jeremiah didn't catch the rest of the sentence. He was thinking too hard about the first part.

Daddy lost his hair! Jeremiah thought. *So that's what this is all about!*

A smile crept across his face. *Well then—I'm going to find it! That will make Daddy very happy.* He scooted off his seat and left the kitchen.

The search for Daddy's hair had begun.

Jeremiah started in the house.
He looked in closets...

cupboards...

and drawers.

He looked in the bathtub.

He looked in the garage.

He even looked in the toilet.... **Nothing.**

Venturing outside, Jeremiah continued his hunt for Daddy's hair. He looked in sewers...

in trash cans...

and under rocks.

He looked in his front yard and the backyard. Even in the garden. Still **nothing**.

He headed back to the house, discouraged.

Where did Daddy's hair go?

Where *would* hair go? And then Jeremiah had an idea. *I wonder if other things lose their hair like Daddy did?*

Jeremiah thought of other things that looked like Daddy's head:

a **pencil eraser**...

a **hill with no grass** on top...

a camel's hump . . .

a turtle, even a **pig**.

Well, maybe the pig and the camel's hump had a little fuzz, but there wasn't a lot of it.

But none of these things really <u>lost</u> their hair, Jeremiah thought. *Some of them didn't even <u>have</u> hair to begin with.*

He sighed and went into the den.

His baby sister, Rosemary, was playing in the crib. Then it hit him.

Rosemary had a smooth, shiny head almost like Daddy's. *Maybe he was just born like that!* Jeremiah thought.

Jeremiah found his father in the backyard.

"Dad," he asked, "were you just born like that?
With no hair?"

"Many people are born nearly bald," replied his dad. "Even you."

"**Yikes!**" Jeremiah felt his head to make sure his hair was still there. "Well, then that's it!"

"No, no. You see, I did eventually grow hair. But as I got older, my hair fell out little by little," Jeremiah's dad explained.

Jeremiah thought about what his father had said. He tried to picture what his dad would look like with hair.

*Would Daddy be a **different person** with hair?* Jeremiah wondered.

"Did it hurt when your hair came out?" Jeremiah asked.
"No."
"Did it bleed?"
"No."

"Did you cry?"
"No," said his dad.
"I was a little upset,
but I realized having
hair doesn't matter.
**It's who you are
on the inside that
really counts.**"

The next day, Jeremiah and his family went to the beach. Jeremiah looked around at the people. They were all different shapes and sizes and colors. Some were small, others TALL. Some skinny, some **fat.**

There were even different kinds of bald heads.
Some looked like doughnuts, others like horseshoes.
Some were completely bald like the man in the moon.

Jeremiah looked over at his dad. The sun was bouncing off his shiny head. Jeremiah smiled. "Daddy," he said.

"Yes, Jeremiah."

"I don't need to look for your hair anymore."

"I think you are **perfect** just the way you are."